Manny

Manny

LILLIAN WHITLOW

ARPress
ILLUMINATING IDEAS,
EMPOWERING VOICES

ARPress LLC
45 Dan Road Suite 5
Canton MA 02021
Hotline: 1(888) 821-0229
Fax: 1(508) 545-7580

Ordering Information:
Quantity sales. Special discounts are available on quantity purchases by corporations, associations, and others. For details, contact the publisher at the address above.

Printed in the United States of America.

ISBN-13:   Softcover   979-8-89356-692-5
            eBook   979-8-89356-693-2

Library of Congress Control Number: 2024904036

Acknowledgments

I am deeply grateful to members of my writers group: MAYA ANGELOU WRITERS GUILD: John Wolfe, O.B. Hill, Emma Ford, D.Norgia Price, Susan Banyas, Nancy Woods, and Mario DePriest.

DEDICATED TO MY CHILDREN

Leo

Leon

Leona

1

THE WINTER OF 1967 in Linton, Oklahoma, was mild, but everyone had wondered what the winter of 1968 would bring.

I was in the backyard one morning, feeding my dog, Buster, when my neighbor hollered across the street.

"Well, I guess we're going to have a bone-chilling winter this year."

"Why?" I asked.

"I heard those wild geese flying over last night honking their heads off. Didn't you hear them?"

She pulled her bulky brown sweater closer to her body and leaned over toward her woodpile against the wall.

"Yes, I did, but it was so late I didn't let them disturb me," I said. "Well, they sure did disturb me. I better get some more firewood to burn in this old house of mine. I don't think the gas will keep me warm all by itself this winter. It's going to need some help."

She gathered a few pieces of wood in the fold of her apron. "Do you think they'll come again?" I asked.

"Some more will be on their way, but those that have already gone by won't be back until spring."

She looked up toward the sky as she spoke with authority, like she'd been around a long time and was an expert on wild geese and the weather. After a few glances backward toward the sky, she shook her head and went inside.

Sure enough, she was right. On December 12, the others did come. The loud screaming honks of those nocturnal fowls woke me as they approached my house. I rolled over to my right side and reached toward the nightstand to turn on the light. I looked at the clock on the wall, and it was 11:42. The screaming honks and cackles grew louder and louder than before, but there was a distinct hoarse honk that soon disappeared among the others.

Flo, my arthritic, cantankerous cat, hobbled into my bedroom, sat in the doorway, and with bewildered eyes, she said, "Madam, something terrible has happened. Those noisy birds are flying above that old pecan tree out there, and I can't sleep." She sat back on her hind legs and waited for a reply.

"All right, Flo. I hear the noise too. Let's see what's out there."

I put my chenille robe around my shoulders, slipped my feet into my house slippers, and walked through the kitchen to the den. Flo hobbled cautiously behind me.

"Don't walk so fast, Madam. You know I can't keep up."

Flo's left hip was stiff, and she could hardly walk at times, especially when it rained. She was middle-aged, and her weight didn't help either. Her overweight gray and white body added to her problems, but she always welcomed food.

When we reached the den, I opened the door and peered out through the glass of the storm door. Flo stood closely behind me, peeping around my robe and purring loudly.

"What is it, Madam?" she panted.

"I don't know, but I see something rustling beneath the tree." I tiptoed above the iron guard on the screen and peered through the glass. "Oh, I see something moving."

Flo moved closer to my leg but stayed safely behind me. "Good gracious, Madam. What is it?" Flo whispered.

"I believe it's a bird, Flo." I looked again and saw a wing flapping. "Yes, it's a bird."

Flo turned back toward the den and hobbled to the sofa. "Well, let's go back to bed, Madam. I need my rest." She was unimpressed.

I looked down at Flo. "We can't, Flo. We can't leave that bird outside to freeze."

She looked up at me with her gray eyes and thick turned-up whiskers. "Yes, we can, Madam." Flo assured me.

"We have to help that bird. Don't you see? If something should happen to you, I would want someone to help you," I pleaded.

"There you go again, Madam. You're just trying to ruin my life."

"I can assure you that I won't ruin your life. I love you. Trust me. Let's go outside and get the bird."

"Then what?" Flo stopped walking. "We'll see if we can help it."

"Leave me out of it, Madam."

2

I OPENED THE door and walked cautiously toward the bird. It lay on its right side, kicking his legs and flapping its wings. Flo stayed inside, looked out the screen door, and watched me lift the bird from the ground. The bird felt cold, and it was shaking from fright or from the weather. I brought it to my chest and caressed it as I walked to the door.

"You're going to be just fine," I said in a soothing voice. "You'll be back on your feet real soon."

This isn't just a bird. It's a wild goose.

I walked toward the house with the goose snuggled to my chest.

The goose was small and fragile. It was a clear night, and the light on the telephone pole gave me enough light to notice that it was wounded, but I didn't know the extent of its injury. I held it in the palm of my hand and carried it inside. The goose was white with a black mark under its neck shaped like a diamond. There was a white band across its throat and cheek and a small black dot on its beak about the size of the head of a straight pin.

"Let's see it, Madam."

"Look," I said and knelt down and held the bird out closer to Flo. "It must have fallen as they flew over the house."

Flo moved back from the bird. "Madam," she said while she slurped and licked her lips, "He's just a mouthful." She slurped again. "Let me at him so I can put him out of his misery. He's so little. It'll only take a few bites," Flo said and turned her head back and forth to estimate its size.

"You can't eat the goose, Flo, and anyway, how do you know that it's a he?"

"They all taste the same, Madam. It doesn't matter with me." She hobbled to the sofa near the back wall. "Help me up on this sofa, Madam. You know I can't get up here by myself," she said in a demanding voice.

"Flo, you can crawl on that stool by the sofa and get on it by yourself. That's why I put it there. You use it every day. Why can't you use it tonight?"

"Oh, Madam. You're so fascinated with that goose. You don't have anymore sympathy for me." Her voice faded into a pitiful whine. "You haven't even noticed that the stool is by your chair where you propped your feet and read your newspaper today."

"I'll move it over there for you." I still held the goose to my chest, while I moved the stool in place for Flo.

As Flo continued to complain, the goose gave out a few feeble honks.

"Listen at him, Madam. He's going to keep me up all night, and I can't get any sleep." She climbed onto the stool and clawed her way onto the sofa. "I have already lost just about an hour of sleep already fooling with that wild goose," she complained.

I held the goose in one hand and helped Flo to the sofa with the other hand. Then I sat down in the soft chair near the sofa and stroked its spiny back with my fingers.

3

F LO SAT UP and glared at the bird. "Now, Madam, what are you going to do with it? It won't stop hollering, and you're not going to get enough sleep so you can get up and make my breakfast in the morning. You know I like to eat early. It helps my arthritis."

"Flo?"

"Yes, Madam." Flo perked up expecting some accommodations. "Close your mouth and go to sleep."

She slumped down, snuggled her fluffy gray body against the stuffed pillow, and turned her face to the wall. "I'm worried about you, Madam," she mumbled. "I don't know what to say about you and that goose. I can take care of that goose with three or four bites, and we both can both get some sleep. Where is it going to sleep tonight, anyway?"

"In the den with you."

Flo forgot her arthritis, drew her head from her pillow, and sat up with her back against the arm on the sofa. "Now wait a minute, Madam," she screamed. "Just wait a minute." She shook her head back and forth. "That's your goose. I can't stand the noise. I'm old. The noise disturbs my arthritis."

"Nonsense, Flo. The goose can't disturb your arthritis. There's a parrot cage in the back bedroom closet. We can put him in the parrot's cage." I rubbed the tiny bird's back again.

"Don't use that word 'we,' Madam. I told you what I could do. I'm trying to help you all I can. I'm good with birds and geese. I wonder

6

why Buster didn't get him before you got him." She looked toward the window near the sofa. "By the way, where's Buster tonight?"

"Buster is probably out somewhere courting."

"This late at night?"

"Dogs don't care about time, Flo." I got up from the chair and walked through the kitchen and to the back bedroom for the cage.

Flo mumbled to herself, "Now that's a smart dog."

I snuggled the goose close to my chest as I went to the bedroom. I could feel the right wing against my arm. The bird began to honk quietly. I stopped and looked at it and discovered that its right wing was bent in half. "Your wing is broken. That's what you've been trying to tell me. I guess I was holding you too close. I'll be careful the next time." I opened the closet door and reached down on the floor and picked up the green, sturdy parrot cage. "You'll sleep in this cage in the den with Flo." I took the bird and the cage back to the den where Flo was asleep. I recognized that it was a wild goose. Perhaps the gaggle was flying south toward warm weather.

"Flo?" I whispered.

Flo turned over. "What is it now, Madam?" she said in a slow drawl.

I set the cage on the small round table beneath the window and put the bird inside the cage. "What do you think, Flo?"

She grunted, stretched her body, and gave a long yawn. "You haven't taken my advice before, Madam, and you're not going to take it now. My offer is still the same. Let me get that goose out of his misery, and let's get some sleep tonight."

"No, you can't do that, Flo."

"I know, Madam. My name is Flo, and I have to go along with the flow."

Flo turned her face toward the wall and grunted. "I'll try to get a little sleep, but take that bird with you to your room," she scowled.

"What can we name it, Flo?"

"Dinner."

"That's not nice," I said. "I think I'll name it Manny. We don't know if it's a male or female, so we'll just name it Manny. How do you like that, Flo?"

Flo began to snore and didn't hear the question. I got a flat stick about two and a half inches long and some string from a drawer beneath the kitchen sink. I lifted the bird out of the cage and secured its right wing by placing it against the stick and winding the string around the wing to the stick. "Manny is going to be your name," I said and put the tiny goose inside the cage. "I have some bird seeds, Manny. I hope you can eat them tonight. Tomorrow I'll go to the store and get some fresh seeds. Those are a little old, but they'll do for the night. I'll give you some water, and you can get some rest too. You've had a long flight, so it's time for a long rest." I put the seeds and water inside the cage.

Manny nibbled at the seeds but refused the water. "I believe he was hungry. Don't you think so, Flo?"

Flo stirred slowly and turned toward me. "Madam, that goose is going to eat everything in sight, and I won't get anything. He's going to get it all."

"You don't eat seeds, so you don't have to worry about that."

"But you won't have any money left to buy my food, Madam. That's what I'm worried about."

"We'll have enough, Flo. I promise."

Flo turned her face to the wall and didn't respond. I went to the kitchen cabinet and took a large white dish towel from a drawer and covered Manny's cage to darken it so he would believe it was night and go to sleep.

4

FTER EVERYTHING WAS under control, I went to my
bedroom, pulled off my robe, slipped out of my house slippers,
and went to bed. The night was still. Cars ceased to travel down
the graveled road, and Buster only barked once at the noise he heard
in the alley.

"Well, he's back," I said. I turned the lights out and fell asleep.

"Meow, meow, meow," Flo said. She hobbled to my bedroom.
"Madam, you must do something. Manny is at it again."

"At what again, Flo?" I sat up in bed. "What is it now?"

"He's disturbing my sleep."

"And you're disturbing mine," I said in annoyance to her petition.
Soon, I heard Manny's honks. They got louder. "What's wrong with
him? What did you do to Manny?"

"Nothing, Madam, but if you give me a chance, just a little bit of
a chance, I can stop that racket." She sat on her back legs favoring her
left side. "Believe me, I have the remedy, and I can stop that honking
and cackling."

"I know you can, Flo," I said as I got up and put my robe on. "Let's
go and see what's wrong with Manny."

Flo followed me to the den where we discovered that the kitchen
towel had slipped off the cage, so Manny thought it was daylight
because the street light on a pole outside the window felled upon his

cage. I covered his cage again and anchored the towel with two books I took from a nearby bookshelf. "Now," I said, "I think that will do until morning."

Flo followed me back to my bedroom. "Flo, you can go back to the den and sleep on the sofa now. I think Manny is going to be just fine."

"That's what you think, Madam. I don't want to trust Manny. I want to sleep in here with you, so you can just move over and let me sleep on the front side."

I impatiently lifted Flo from the floor and placed her behind me. "No, you can sleep behind me."

I pulled the cover up to her neck and patted it around her neck to make sure that she was warm and would stay that way.

"I don't like being on the back side, Madam," she mumbled.

"Flo, this is my bed. You're just a guest. Remember?"

"Humph," she said and reluctantly turned her back and faced the wall.

After the adjustments with Manny and Flo were made, the night was still, warm, and comfortable inside. The next morning, the sun shone brightly through the window curtains. Flo sat up in the bed and looked around, licked her front paws, and rubbed them over her face.

"Good gracious," she said. With eyes wide open, she looked at the clock above the window. "It's eight o'clock. I'm two hours late for my breakfast. That bird is going to starve me to death. Get up, Madam. Get up," she demanded as she nudged me in the back with her paws. "Get up. It's time for my breakfast. I got to potty too." She pushed the cover from her body and attempted to crawl over me to the floor.

"All right, Flo. I'm getting up," I said. I put both feet on the floor, put my robe around my shoulders, and eased into my house slippers. "Let me help you down."

Flo came toward me to be lifted and placed on the floor. I took her to the back door and let her out to potty. "I'll let you in when I'm dressed. Flo."

Manny was still quiet. As I walked from the bathroom. I heard Flo scratching on the back door. I opened it and let her in. "Now I'm ready for my breakfast, Madam."

"I'll feed you as soon as I can, and then I'll feed Buster. Manny has enough food left from last night."

"Well, make it soon," Flo demanded.

5

BUSTER, WITH HIS dusty, shaggy brown body, lay on his back snuggled in a deep bed of dry leaves beneath the pecan tree. He didn't belong to any specific breed. Buster was a mixture of many breeds. He was midsize, with white markings through his brown fur. He was gentle, fearless, and didn't have a care in the world. All Buster wanted to do was eat, sleep, and prowl at night. Manny was Flo's worry—not his.

When Flo came inside, she looked back at Buster grudgingly. "Oh, for the life of a dog. After going through what I went through last night with Manny, I'd give eight of my nine lives for the life of Buster."

"Flo, stop complaining. You slept very well." I took the towel off of Manny's cage so he could see the daylight. He began to honk. "I know you're hungry too, Manny, and we're all going to eat in a little while." I walked over to the kitchen sink, washed my hands, and dried them on a paper towel beneath the top cabinet.

"You don't have to do all of that. I'm already two hours late with my breakfast, Madam. I can't wait any longer."

Manny began to honk loudly again. "I'll get your breakfast in a little while, Manny."

"Manny, Manny, Manny. That's all you can think about is Manny," Flo sneered as she looked up at Madam. "You'll have to wait, Flo, so just go down in the den and wait until I call you to breakfast."

Flo turned and hobbled toward the den. "I don't know what's happening to you, Madam. I believe you're losing your mind since Manny came here. I know he's driving me out of mine," she grumbled on her way to the den.

I took fresh water and a cup of seeds for Manny. Manny was a slow eater, but he was eager as I opened his cage.

"SS TW," Flo said and sat up on the sofa. "You're feeding Manny first? I told you I was already two hours late, Madam. I thought you weren't going to feed him now." She called from the den.

"I changed my mind. But you're next, after I feed Buster."

"It's about time. You promise?"

"Yes, I promise." I reached under the kitchen cabinet and got a can of dog food for Buster, opened it, put it in a pan, and carried it outside to him. When I came inside, I got a three-ounce can of cat food from under the cabinet and placed it under the can opener. When Flo heard the can opener, she rushed to the kitchen as fast as she could and stood near the table.

"It's about time. Is that mine? It smells like it."

"Yes, this is yours."

"What are you fixing for yourself, Madam?" She brushed back and forth against my legs with her large body.

"Two slices of bacon, two eggs, two pieces of toast, and a cup of coffee."

"Oh boy, when?"

"As soon as I get you fed."

"Well, on second thought," she ran her tongue over mouth and smacked her lips, "I'll take some of that too."

"I don't think so. That's not cat food."

"I can live another day without eating cat food, Madam."

"It's already cut, so I'll put it in your pan."

"What about water?"

"You'll get that too, Flo. I always give you water with your food."

"I don't know about you, Madam." She shook her head and began to nibble at her food. She lifted her head from her pan and noticed that I had sat at the table with my plate of bacon, eggs, toast, and coffee.

"When did you fix that, Madam?"

"When I was preparing yours and Manny's."

The aroma of the fried bacon overwhelmed Flo, so she left her pan of food and water on the floor and came to the table. She pulled herself up to my knee with her front paws. "I like your food better, Madam. I'm tired of that old cat food. That's all you give me," she grumbled. "I want some eggs, bacon, and toast. Now you can keep that coffee for yourself."

I broke a half of a slice of bacon and took a teaspoon of eggs and put them on Flo's pan with her other food. "Now you can eat this with your own breakfast, and I'll eat mine."

Flo looked at the small portion I put in her pan. "You're getting stingy, Madam," she complained. She crawled down from my knee. "I don't know what I'm going to do with you."

"You'll think of something, Flo. You always do." After she finished eating the piece of bacon and egg, she came to the table and put her front paws on my knee again.

I lifted her from the floor and rubbed her back. "You'll make it." I patted her on her head.

"That feels so good, Madam." She pressed her head to my chest for more.

"You shouldn't feel that Manny is taking your place, Flo. He's just here for a short time, but you're here forever. Remember, you have nine lives." I laughed.

Flo pushed back and looked up at me wide-eyed. "Not anymore, Madam, not anymore."

"Why not?"

"Why not? Manny has already taken eight of them."

I laughed. "Manny will soon be strong enough to fly again, and then he will join his gaggle of geese."

"When? When is he going home?" Flo whispered as to not disturb Manny.

"I don't know, but as soon as his wings are healed and he's strong enough to fly, he'll join his gaggle."

"Will they know him?"

"Of course. He's larger and stronger now, but they'll recognize him. How can they ever forget Manny with that hoarse honk?"

"Easily," Flo said for fear they might have to keep Manny.

6

FOR DAYS AND weeks, Manny and Flo continued to test each other. Manny seemed to have enjoyed irritating Flo by honking loudly when he saw her relaxing on the sofa. Flo constantly screamed, "Aw, hush your fuss, Manny."

Manny's wing had healed enough for me to remove the flat stick and string, and I felt that he might be strong enough to fly around inside the den. I took him outside of his cage for a flight test. I placed him on my left arm and pushed him upward. Manny flew from the cage and landed on the soft green chair near the kitchen door. He flapped his wings and gave out a loud honk.

"Sounds like he's scared, Madam." Flo sat up on the divan with her mouth agape while she observed Manny.

"You can do it, Manny. Keep trying," I said. I stood near him and placed my hand on his quivering back. He was so afraid. His eyes were wide as he looked up in despair.

Manny's honks got louder. He didn't know how to fly from the soft chair. "You'll fail sometimes, Manny, but if you keep trying, you'll get better and better. You might fail again and again, but someday, you'll get better, and you'll be on your own." I placed Manny inside his cage. "We'll try again soon. All right, Manny?"

"I know he can make it, Madam. Manny is strong enough to go home."

"I don't think so," I said, and I sat down in the big soft chair. "I think he'll be ready by December though."

"December?" Flo shouted. "That's almost a whole year from now."

"Not quite. Six months at the most. It's June now, and I believe he can join the gaggle when they fly over again in December."

"That's still a long time," Flo muttered. "But how do you know they'll be back in December? How can you be sure, Madam?"

"They always do, Flo."

"I hope they won't forget Manny," she meowed and walked toward the sofa.

"They won't. I promise."

"I've heard that before, Madam. I'm going to take a nap while I can. You never can tell when Manny is going to start his music again."

Flo lay down on the sofa, turned her face toward the wall, and went to sleep.

The weather was humid and extremely warm. The pecan tree branches had shaded the ground beneath its base. Buster lay on his back in the shade under the tree with his head turned toward the door. His back feet were up and his front feet fell across his chest.

After Flo's short nap, she sat up, stretched, and looked around. "You're still there. Madam?" She asked rubbing her eyes.

"Yes, and that was a short nap you had," I said.

"It was just a catnap, Madam. I need a lot of those during the day because with Manny in the house as your guest, I don't get much rest at night. He's just a guest. Isn't he?"

"Stop complaining, Flo."

Flo crawled down from the sofa and went to the door and looked out at Buster and stared at him while he lay relaxing in the shade.

"Oh, for the life of a dog. What a life." She sat back leaning to her right side and starred out at Buster.

"Do you like Buster's life?"

She turned and looked at me. "Just for one day, Madam."

7

"**Y**OU WON'T HAVE to worry about Manny too long because he'll be strong enough to fly with the best of the wild geese. I want Manny to take the apex when they fly over in December."

Flo rubbed her paw across her face and looked at me. "What's the apex, Madam?"

"An apex is where the leader positions himself to fly. The wild geese fly in a 'V' formation. The leader takes the pointed form of the formation, and some of the other geese form a line to the left of the leader and the others form a line to the right, and that is the way they fly to their destination. That's the way they will fly in December. You'll see," I said, shaping my arms in the shape of a "V."

She shook her head. "Sounds like you have a lot of confidence in that goose."

"Manny. His name is Manny," I corrected. "He's still a goose."

Manny's wing was completely healed, and he was physically strong, but he lacked the confidence to fly. The crash he had when he fell beneath the tree six months ago still overwhelmed him.

I must convince Manny that he'll be just fine, I thought. *He's supposed to fly.* "Flo, if I let Manny out of his cage, will you look after him?"

I waited for her reply while she lay relaxed on the sofa.

Flo sat up with a sheepish grin on her face. "Yes, Madam, I'll look after him all right."

"That's not what I mean, Flo. I want you to see that he doesn't get hurt. He can fly around in the den. If he gets into trouble, let me know."

"Where're you going, Madam?"

"In the living room. I want to read the morning paper," I said. "It's afternoon and I still haven't read the paper." In the meantime, I raised the window higher near the sofa, leaving the iron bars across the window exposed.

"All right. Let him out, Madam."

"Will you behave?"

"It'll be hard, but I'll do my best." She entertained herself with a smug look. "Uh, Madam?"

"Yes?"

"Will you fix me some bacon, eggs, and toast in the morning?" I recognized the bribe. "If you like," I said.

"I like, Madam."

I opened the cage and took Manny out. I placed him on my arm and gave him an upward lift. "Now, Manny, you'll have to practice on your own. Flo will watch after you."

"Honk, honk, honk," Manny responded and gave Flo the I-bet-you-will look.

"Honk back to you," Flo said. "I don't like this any better than you, but I have to do what I have to do."

When Manny began to flutter around in the den, I went to the living room to read. Manny felt confident enough to fly into the living room and perch on my shoulder.

"Manny, you're supposed to be practicing how to fly again. I see you're doing quite well, but you're supposed to be in the den with Flo." I gave him a soft pat on his head.

Manny brushed his beak against my face as I talked to him. "I know you're going to miss us, and we're going to miss you too, but you have to go back to your gaggle this winter. They'll be expecting you to return in sound body and mind." I took Manny back to the den.

"He wanted to go to the living room with you, Madam," Flo said when I entered the den with Manny. "He can fly. I saw him fly to the living room. Why, he just flapped his wings and flew in the living room, no trouble at all."

"I know he can, but he doesn't know how well he can fly. We have to convince him that he can fly too." I looked at Manny who had perched on the iron bars on the window. "You have to be careful, Manny," I warned. "You can fall between those bars." Manny gave out a defiant honk and remained perched on the iron bars. The window was raised high, and the gently breeze blew the white sheer curtains back and forth in front of Manny.

Flo stretched out on the sofa to take her afternoon nap. "He'll be all right, Madam. Go on and read. That breeze feels so good."

"Are you sure you can handle everything, Flo?"

"Sure, Madam. Leave everything to me." She lay back on the sofa.

8

I WALKED HESITANTLY to the living room to recline on the sofa. It was four o'clock. I thought I could read, take a short nap, and prepare dinner about six o'clock. With the exception of a few cars heard driving down the street, the afternoon was quiet until . . . Just as I reclined on the sofa and opened my paper, I heard loud meows and honks from the den.

Before I could walk to the kitchen, Flo hobbled up from the den and into the living room. Her eyes were wide with fright. "Hurry, Madam," she said and turned back toward the kitchen to the den. "Manny is inside the window. I don't know how he did it, but he's between the bars and the screen. Hurry," she summoned and walked away.

When I went to Manny, he was between the bars and the screen, with his head touching the raised window. His back was pressed against the screen, and his beak and neck were raised just above the rim of the bar. His eyes were opened wide with fright, and his beak also opened wide, allowing rapid honks to escape.

Manny's honks got louder and louder. He was more afraid than he was when he fell below the pecan tree in December.

"Just be quiet, Manny. I'll get you out of this somehow."

I went to the kitchen and opened a drawer where I kept some small tools. I look out a large screwdriver and rushed back to Manny.

"What's that, Madam?"

"Screwdriver," I said and held it up. "Will it work?"

"We'll see." I unscrewed the twelve screws that held the bar to the window and lifted Manny out. Again, I held him to my breast and caressed him. "You're going to get better, Manny. You have to keep trying, but be careful. Watch your surroundings, and you can avoid being hurt again."

Manny whimpered a few more honks. I placed him inside his cage. "You can stay here for a while. When you're ready to come out again, let me know."

Flo climbed down from the sofa and sat trembling in front of the table beneath Manny's cage. "I was so afraid for Manny, Madam. Do you think he'll try to fly again?"

"Not soon, but he will some day. Right now, he's afraid to try, but he will."

"I'll stay right here and watch him. I was asleep when it happened. Maybe I shouldn't have gone to sleep. Maybe if I had been looking after him, he wouldn't have gotten hurt."

"You shouldn't blame yourself, Flo. Manny will perhaps have a few more falls before he can join the flock in December. You did a good job." I knelt down and stroked Flo's back. "You're a good goose watcher."

"I'll be a better watcher from now on, Madam. You can go back to the living room and read."

"I notice how careful you are with Manny. You don't want to eat him anymore."

"Now don't tempt me, Madam." She stretched out and lay closely beneath Manny's cage.

I didn't know whom to pity the most—Manny or Flo. Manny was afraid to fly, and Flo felt guilty for Manny's failure. However, it was a good sign because Flo had become concerned about Manny's well-being. He saw Manny as an annoyance, an acceptable companion, rather than just a goose to eat. However, they continued to test and annoy each other during the summer months.

9

T HE SUMMER MONTHS were almost over. I took Manny outside daily to strengthen her injured wing. With a string tied to one leg, she could fly the height of the pecan tree, perch on the top branch, and flap her wings. Flo always came for the rehearsal.

"I believe he'll fly someday, Madam."

"I know he will." I held the string and extended it so Manny could fly to the top of pecan tree, but he was satisfied with just sitting on the top branches. Toward the end of summer, Manny had begun to fly several feet above the pecan tree. One day, he was so confident that he flew between the top branches and got tangled between the branches. I tugged at the string lightly to untangle him, but he was stuck beyond my help. He hung upside down with his head pointed to the ground. His wings spread full length and his feet stretched upward. Manny had always cried out when he was in trouble, but this time, he was too afraid to make a sound.

"What can we do now, Madam?" Flo asked.

"Stay here and watch him. I'll tie the string around the trunk of the tree and go for help."

"Where?"

"Next door. Mr. Tindel has a ladder, and I believe he can reach Manny because he is also tall."

"But Mr. Tindel is old, Madam."

"He's not too old to get on the ladder."

"He's still old, Madam."

"Don't say that, Flo. He's only about fifty. He can climb a ladder. That's why he has one."

"He's still old, Madam."

"He's all we've got, Flo, so you just stay here and wait. I'll be back soon with Mr. Tindel." I went next door, and Mrs.Tindel came to the door. She was a short, plumb woman about fifty. She always had something funny to say or to laugh about something that had happened recently.

"Mrs. Tindel, I have a problem," I sighed, "and I need Mr. Tindel to help with his ladder."

"What's the problem?" she asked. "Come on in," she beckoned while she held the screen door open.

"My wild goose, Manny, you remember him?" I said as I entered the door.

"Manny keeps getting into something. What has he gotten into now?" She laughed.

"Flo and I took him outside to see if he could fly, and he got tangled at the top of the tree, and he's hanging upside down."

Mrs. Tindel laughed harder. "Manny has gotten into a lot of difficulties since he's been in captivity. Maybe he's trying to test himself."

"He is doing that, and he's also testing me and Flo."

"I'll go back into the kitchen and tell Mark. He'll bring his ladder over and get Manny down. Why don't you sit there on the sofa," she gestured.

"I appreciate that, Mrs. Tindel, but I'll go back and see about Flo and Manny. I'll be in the backyard waiting, Mrs. Tindel."

"He'll be there soon," she promised as I left to go home.

Mr. Tindel came to backyard with his twenty-foot ladder by his side. With his tall thin body, he carried the twelve-foot ladder by his side and walked toward the tree. I was satisfied that he could do the job. He was agile for his age and seemed able to climb a ladder.

"Hi there," he said when he entered the gate. "Good evening, Mr. Tindel."

He looked up toward Manny, shaded his eyes with one hand, and watched Manny flap his wings back and forth. "I see you've got quite a problem, but I can fix it."

He placed his ladder against the tree and steadied it and climbed slowly up the ladder toward Manny. Manny honks grew louder and louder as he approached him.

"I'm not going to hurt you," he said. "I'm going to get you down so you can do this again," he teased.

"I hope not," I said. Manny wasn't convinced that Mr. Tindel wasn't going to hurt him. He moved his wings slightly and honked faintly.

"Madam, do you think he knows that Mr. Tindel is going to help him?"

"No, Flo, but he'll soon know. Mr. Tindel is almost up there."

"Manny," Mr. Tindel called to him in a soft and calm tenor voice, "you're going to be fine. I'm not going to hurt you. Let me help you." He reached his hands out to Manny. "See," he said without touching Manny. "I'm not going to hurt you, but you have to trust me."

Manny stopped flapping his wings.

Mr. Tindel touched Manny's head. "You're a good bird. I know you are, but you just keep getting into the wrong places." He took Manny in both hands and then transferred him to his right hand. He climbed backward slowly down the ladder with Manny held close to his chest.

"Here's your bird, Madam," he said and handed Manny to me. "Thank you, Mr. Tindel. I don't know what we would have done without your help." I held Manny close to me and stroked his back. "That's all right, Manny. We'll try again. Thank you again, Mr. Tindel."

"Oh, that's all right. Manny is trying to help himself, but he'll soon get it together. I know he will," Mr. Tindel said. "If you need me again, let me know."

"Thank you again," I said.

"You're welcome," he said and took his ladder and left.

"I still believe he can fly, Madam. I still believe he can really fly," Flo said.

"I do too. I know he can fly, but we will keep trying."

10

MANNY WAS STILL cautious. He would only fly around from chair to chair in the den, dining room, and kitchen. It took at least three months for him to build up his confidence to fly into the living room, but the summer months ended, and an early fall began. Manny had to be ready to go with the gaggles when they arrived in December.

"Do you think Manny is going to be ready to leave in December, Madam?" Flo asked one morning.

"Sure, he will. He just has to keep trying."

"Well, you need to get out the Christmas decoration, Madam."

"I guess it's about that time." I continued to wash the breakfast dishes.

"You can wash the dishes later," Flo said as she leaned back on her right leg in the doorway to the den.

"We have plenty of time, Flo. It's not Thanksgiving yet. It's the middle of October."

"I like the red and green lights, Madam."

"We can put them up before the weekend. I believe Manny will like the bright lights too. This will be his last Christmas with us," I said.

"Are you sure he'll go home, Madam?"

"Of course, he will. He might be ready to leave before Christmas."

"But he might not be ready, Madam, and you shouldn't make him leave if he's not ready to leave."

"Would you?"

"I thought you wanted him to go." I dried my hands on the dishcloth and hung it on the wall near the cabinet. "Let's sit in the den with Manny." I stepped down into the den with Flo following behind me. I sat on the soft chair near the door, while Flo sat on the floor beneath Manny's cage. Manny sat on his swing in the cage, still too petrified to move. Fear seemed to linger with him. Although he fell between the bar and window months before, fear seemed to visit him often. Of course, getting tangled at the top of the pecan tree didn't help his confidence. Flo moved away from the doorway and looked up at Manny in his cage. "Manny has gotten too big for his cage, Madam. Look at his head. It's touching the top of the cage, and his wings are too big to spread out," she gestured with both front arms. "He might be too big to fly. I believe you fed him too much, Madam."

"I fed him enough, Flo. You sound like you don't want to see Manny go. You wanted to eat him the first time you saw him, remember?"

Embarrassed by the thought, Flo stretched out on the floor beneath Manny's cage. "That was then, Madam," she said. "But you see," she purred, "he kind of grew on me."

"You mean you like him now."

"I guess you can say I'm getting there."

Manny looked down at Flo and began to honk and cackle. He then began to bounce up and down on the swing out of frustration.

"Now what's wrong with him, Madam?"

"I believe he wants to get out," I said.

"No, I believe he would appreciate a Christmas tree."

Manny doesn't know anything about Christmas, Flo. I believe you are the one who wants the Christmas tree."

"I'll go along with that, Madam," she said. "I like to see the shiny star on top of the tree.

"Well," I said, "I guess Manny will have to see the Christmas tree before he leaves, so I'll get it from the back closet and set it up."

"Where?" Flo asked.

"Where we always put it—in the living room by the picture window."

"Do you need my help, Madam?" Flo asked.

"No, you just sit there on the sofa and watch. It won't take long. It's not a big tree."

"It's big enough, Madam." Flo climbed on the sofa. "Let's hurry so Manny can see it before he leaves us."

"I'm hurrying as fast as I can," I said. I went to the back bedroom for the tree and ornaments. When I brought them up to the living room, I put the branches on the tree and placed it in front of the window. I placed red, green, and yellow satin balls on the branches and draped the tree in icicles. The Christmas tree was only four feet tall, just tall enough for our small family.

"Don't forget the star, Madam," Flo warned.

I put the small shiny silver star at the top of the tree at Flo's request. "That looks good, Madam. Now when Manny comes in December again, he will see the shiny star and know that he's home again."

"Do you consider this Manny's home?"

"This will always be Manny's home," Flo said.

I stood by the tree and admired it. "I guess I'd better get Manny and let him see the tree. What do you think?"

"Do that, Madam." Flo crawled down from the sofa. "I'll just sit here in front of the tree and wait."

11

I WENT TO the den and got Manny out of his cage. "Come with me, Manny," I said and held him close to me. "I have a surprise." Manny's body trembled, and he fluttered his wings against my chest.

"You don't need to be afraid of anything, Manny. You're going to be just fine. I promise."

When we reached the living room, Flo was sitting about five feet from the tree. "Are you getting a good look at the tree, Flo?"

"Yes, Madam. We see the tree every year, but it's always a new experience for me." She looked up admiring the tree.

"I'm going to put Manny on the back of the sofa, and you can look after him while I go back to the den and finish ironing.

"Go ahead, Madam. I'll watch Manny. Won't I, Manny?" She looked up at Manny perched on the back of the sofa. "You go right ahead, Madam. We'll be all right. Won't we, Manny?"

Manny moved back and forth sideways on the sofa. "I guess he's doing a little dance, Madam."

"No." I laughed. "He's still thinking about the pecan tree." I went to the den to iron a few kitchen curtains. There was a long silence, and then I heard a swoosh sound. I stopped and listened again. It was silent. *Oh well*, I thought. *Everything is all right up there in the living room*, so I continued to iron.

"Oh, Madam, come here, come here," Flo summoned. "You have to hurry," she shrieked.

I rushed to the living room. "What's wrong?" I saw the tree on the floor about one foot from Flo. Where's Manny?" I asked.

"Oh boy, oh boy," she cried.

"Under the tree," she pointed. "I was looking at the tree when Manny flew into the tree, and it fell right here in front of me, Madam," she pointed down toward her hind feet with her front paws. Flo was too afraid to move. "Manny's going to take this last life I have left before he leaves." Manny lay motionless on his back. The Christmas tree had pinned him to the floor with the star by his head. I lifted the tree upward.

Manny still held on to one of the tree branches. This time, he was too afraid to make a sound and too afraid to release the branch.

"Manny," I said, "what do you have against trees?" I carefully removed him from the tree. "You fell beneath the pecan tree last year, you got tangled at the top of the pecan tree, and now you got tangled in the Christmas tree. Are you hurt?"

"Are you hurt?" Flo mimicked. "What about me?" She brushed her front paws against her chest. "What about me?"

"You are all right, Flo. But we want Manny to be ready to go with his flock when they arrive, so he can't suffer any more failures.

I caressed Manny and cautioned him about the tree. "Just look at the Christmas tree, Manny. Don't go near it," I warned him. I placed him on the back of the living room sofa again.

"Do you think Manny understands what you're saying, Madam?"

"I hope so because I need to finish my work in the den."

Manny flew off the back of the sofa and perched on the bedroom door that was left ajar. He began to make sounds of despair. He honked and honked, and his honks got louder.

"Aw, hush your fuss, Manny. You've done enough for one day."

"Stay with him, Flo. I'll be through ironing soon, and then I'll prepare some dinner. How do you like that?" I walked through the dining room to the den.

"I'll go along with that, Madam." She climbed onto the sofa. "I got down off the sofa to get a good look at the tree. I guess Manny wanted to do the same thing."

"He's still trying," I said.

"When are we going to take him outside again, Madam?"

"I don't think he's ready now." I proceeded to go to the den. "Aw, Madam," Flo scowled, "you can do that anytime."

"Flo, you can stay in the living room with Manny just for a while longer."

"If you say so, Madam."

"If we're going to take Manny outside, I'll have to put a string on his leg again to see that he doesn't get too far if he can fly, but I don't think he's ready for that now," I called back to her.

"I don't think so either, Madam," she said with a sigh of relief.

December 10 was the trial date for Manny's next attempt to try to fly. I had marked it on the calendar on the wall near the kitchen table. Regardless of the weather, Manny would have his next attempt to fly.

12

ONE EVENING, AFTER dinner, I took Flo to the kitchen and showed her the date on the calendar. "What do you think, Flo?"

"About what?"

"The date I have circled on the calendar."

"Is this a guessing game, Madam?"

"No. I circled December 10 for Manny to try to fly again. This time, he'll try outside."

"Oh, Madam, are you out of your mind? Suppose he flies away?" she scowled.

"I'll put a long string on his leg as I did before, and he can just go so far."

I went to the kitchen and got a ball of string from a drawer and tied a string securely around one of Manny's legs. "I believe we can go outside now, Flo."

"I hope you know what you're doing, Madam." She followed me as we went outside.

I tied the end to the string around my left arm and made sure that the string was loose and long enough to give Manny a wide range to fly.

I stood away from the tree while Flo stood behind me. I placed Manny on my left arm and bounced him up into the air. Manny flew atop of the naked pecan tree and perched on a strong limb.

"You can fly, Manny. Get off the tree branch. Let's see how far you can fly." I tugged lightly at the string.

Manny flew down and perched on my shoulder and honked.

"I know you can fly, Manny. You have only a few days left before the flock comes this way. I believe it will be real soon. You must fly away with them."

Manny honked and cackled until I took him inside and put him inside his cage. "You'll be all right, Manny. I know you will."

I didn't take Manny out of his cage the next day because I thought he had enough traumas for a day. We followed the same routine around the house as far as eating, house cleaning, and reading the newspaper. I had marked December 12 on the calendar for Manny's departure, and I was determined that that would be the day.

When the date arrived, I opened the door late at night to get a feel of the weather. The night was bitter cold, but the sky was clear; and the light on the telephone pole in the backyard lit up the yard. The full moon also lit up the sky. I closed the door quietly because Flo was already asleep on the sofa. I tiptoed up into the kitchen to my bedroom and dressed for bed. We were already asleep when we heard the honks and cackles.

Flo hobbled to my bedroom. "Madam, I hear them," she said sadly. "I believe that's the flock of geese that came last December. What do you think?" I said.

"Sounds like it to me. Manny recognizes them too, Madam. Don't you hear him trying to answer them?" Manny gave out some weak honks under his covered cage.

I listened for a while. "Yes, I hear him. He must recognize their honks." I put my robe on and slid my feet into my slippers. "Let's go and get Manny, Flo."

"What do you think he'll do, Madam?"

"We'll soon find out."

"Where's the string?" Flo asked.

"I'm not going to use any string tonight. He'll have to do it on his own. If he's ever going to fly, now is the time." The honks got closer. I took Manny out of his cage. "Manny, they're here," I whispered softly to him. You must show them how strong you are and how big you have grown. You must take the apex if they need a leader."

"Don't they already have a leader, Madam?" Flo asked. "Maybe not. That's why they're coming here."

I opened the door and held Manny close to my face. "Don't forget what I said, Manny. You must take the apex."

13

OUR EXPECTED GUESTS hovered above and around the tree and wouldn't go away. I opened the screen door wide. "Let's go outside, Flo."

We went outside and waited about ten seconds. The flock had scattered and hovered above our house. I held Manny close to me, not wanting to let go, but I knew that Manny had to join his gaggle. I knew that he was strong enough to be a leader. I knew he could lead his flock to a warmer place and to a feeding ground. The sky was clear, the full moon was huge and bright, and there was only one clear azure cloud. The way was clear for Manny. Buster came running down the alley and into the yard and stood to my left side, while Flo stood to my right. They both sat back on their hind legs to watch Manny take flight.

My neighbor came out of her back door. "Do you think he's going to fly?" she asked.

"I know he's going to fly. I know he can do it," I said. "I believe he can too."

"It's time, Manny," I whispered. "There's no string attached now so you can fly high. Take the apex and have a good flight." I bounced Manny up toward the flock. The geese rejoiced with their loud honks and cackles. I stood behind Flo and Buster while they leaned back on their hind legs looking up at Manny.

"They're glad to see Manny, Madam."

"I believe they are," I said.

Buster gave a pleasant growl and sat back on his hind legs.

Manny soared up among the geese and let them inspect him, and then he flew above them as if he was going to lead them away. The flock gathered in a "V" formation behind him, giving out cheerful honks and cackles, but Manny began to honk and cackle. He swirled around and flew down toward us.

"No, no, Manny," I said as I waved my arms wildly forward. "Go on. You must go on."

The wild geese became disoriented and flew around in a circle. "You can do it, Manny."

"What is he going to do, Madam?"

"He's going to fly." I continued to wave my arm forward. "Go on, Manny. You can do it. I know you can."

14

MANNY FLEW IN a semicircle and soared upward toward a lonely cloud. With stretched out wings and grace of a pro, he flew to the apex with great speed and control. When he reached the cloud, he flapped his wings backward, stretched them full length, and soared above the azure cloud. The gaggle regrouped in a "V" formation behind Manny and followed him above and beyond the cloud, cackling gleefully.

Flo looked up at the geese in awe. "Did you see that, Madam?"

"See what?" I asked.

"They flew up like magic," Flo said.

"I saw that too, Flo. It has been said that when each goose flaps its wings, it creates an uplift for the other that follows."

"That's magic, Madam."

"Yes, it is." I stood looking up toward the sky and hoping to hear just a sound from Manny.

"I don't see them anymore, Madam."

Buster barked and wagged his tail. He seemed satisfied that Manny was well and on his way home.

"I believe he's going to make it," my neighbor said. "I know he is."

"Can you hear them?" Flo asked. "Just a little."

There was a final hoarse honk, and then there was silence. "Will he come again, Madam?" Flo's voice cracked.

"Of course, he will."

"When?"

"Probably next December."

"Won't he be in bird heaven by that time?"

"No. Manny can live about sixty more years if he's careful."

"He can?"

"Sure."

"Then we'll see him again next year?"

"Of course, we will."

We stood in the silence for a few moments, and then Flo and I went inside the house, and my neighbor went inside her house. Buster bowed his head and lay slowly on his belly under the pecan tree.

www.ingramcontent.com/pod-product-compliance
Lightning Source LLC
Chambersburg PA
CBHW071215300726
48975CB00004B/1322